Written by Karen Gedig Burnett • Illustrated by Laurie Barrows

SIMON'S Hook

A story about teases and put-downs

a grandma rose story

FISH SCHOOL

GR PUBLISHING
FELTON, CA 95018

© 2000 by GR Publishing
Felton, CA 95018
www.grandmarose.com

Illustrations © 1999 Laurie Barrows

Cover design: Tamara Dever, TLC Graphics, Austin, TX

Burnett, Karen Gedig.
       Simon's hook : a story about teases and put downs/
written by Karen Gedig Burnett; illustrated by Laurie Barrows. — 1st ed.
       p. cm.
       LCCN: 99-71709
       ISBN-13: 978-0-9668530-0-1 (hardcover)
       ISBN-13: 978-0-9668530-1-8 (softcover)
       SUMMARY: When Simon's bad haircut makes him the target
of teasing, Grandma Rose teaches him how to refuse to "take the hook"
by using skillful interpersonal communication techniques.

       1. Teasing—Juvenile fiction. 2. Self-help techniques—
Juvenile fiction. 3. Interpersonal communication in children—
Juvenile fiction. I. Barrows, Laurie. II Title.

PZ7.B93412Si 1999   [E]

                        QBI99-524

10 9 8

Printed in Hong Kong through Creative Printing USA and Morris Press Ltd

to my
mother and father,
Phyllis and John

From you I learned
my basic lessons in life.

It was a bad hair day for Simon.
First his sister lost her gum.
Then she found it ... in his hair.
When she tried to fix it, she went
SNIP SNIP and a big chunk of his
hair was gone.

He grabbed his hat and ran outside,
hoping no one would see.

And no one did see ... until Simon fell and lost his hat.
That's when Joey yelled, "What happened to your hair?"
Everybody turned to look.
"Who cut it?" Nicole asked.
"What did they use, a lawn mower?"
Miguel said as he laughed.

"Hey, Lawn Mower Head!" Joey said.
Simon grabbed his hat and started to leave.
"I've got to go home," he said as he stomped away.
"I've got chores to do."
"Don't forget to cut the lawn," said Nicole.
Everyone laughed — everyone but Simon.

Simon ran and ran.
He ran until he couldn't
see his friends anymore.
"Why do they
make fun of me?" he yelled.
"Why don't they just
LEAVE ME ALONE!"

Simon was so mad he didn't see Grandma Rose ...
until he ran into her.
"Whoa!" she cried. "What's the hurry?"
"I'm going home," Simon cried.
"Why?" asked Grandma Rose.
"What's wrong?"
"I'm having a bad day,"
said Simon, "a bad hair day."
"What's wrong with
your hair?" she asked.

Simon took off his hat.
"Oh," said Grandma Rose. "I see."
Simon told her about the gum and his sister's hair cut.
Then he told her what happened at the park.
"Mmmm, that's too bad," she said.
"Yeah, and they'll tease me again,"
said Simon. "And I don't
know what to do."
Grandma Rose shook her head.
"You do have a problem."
Then she asked him
something really strange.
"But why do you bite?"
"Bite?" cried Simon.
"I didn't bite anyone!"
"No, no, no.
That's not what I mean.
I know you didn't
bite anyone," she said.
"What I mean is …
well … wait here.
I'll be back in a minute."

Grandma Rose disappeared into her garage.
When she returned she was wearing a fishing outfit.
On the end of her fishing line was a piece of paper.

"You see, Simon," Grandma Rose said as she cast out her line, "when people tease you it's like they're throwing out a hook to see if you'll chase it and bite."
"Ohhhhh," Simon said as he watched the hook fly through the air.
"Now I see what you're doing. This is a lesson."
"That's right," said Grandma Rose with a wink.
"It's a ... fishing lesson."

"Today they made fun of your hair," she said
as she dangled the hook in front of Simon.
"They called you Lawn Mower Head,
and you bit." "I sure did," he said.
"Well then," said Grandma Rose,
"grab the hook."

Grandma Rose pulled Simon around the patio. "I've caught you," she said. "You're not a free fish anymore." "But what else can I do?" cried Simon as he flew through the yard.

Grandma Rose put her fishing pole aside and sat down.
"Well, I know a story that might help," she said.
"It's a fish story. Would you like to hear it?"
"Sure," said Simon.
Grandma Rose took a sip
of lemonade and began to talk.

So they talked to the older fish. They talked to the sea creatures too. They asked questions. They took notes. They studied hooks and they learned.

The first idea they had was to DO VERY LITTLE or NOTHING.
DON'T REACT to the hooks.

The second idea they had was to AGREE with the hooks.

The fourth idea was to LAUGH or JOKE about the hooks.

And the fifth idea was to STAY AWAY.
Swim in another part of the sea.

Now the fish don't bite. They don't even chase hooks.

Grandma Rose leaned back and smiled.
"And that's how the fish learned to stay free," she said.
Simon thought. He thought about the hooks and the fish.
He thought about how the fish learned not to bite.
Then he said, "They can tease me all they want.
I won't bite. I'm going to be a FREE FISH too!"
"Good for you," said Grandma Rose.

Simon jumped up and ran to the playground.
He couldn't wait for someone to say something about his hair.
He didn't have to wait long.
As Simon ran up someone yelled,
"Hey, Lawn Mower Head is back!"
"Yep, I'm back," said Simon.

"How's the hair?" Miguel asked.
"It's still on my head," said Simon,
"at least what's left of it."
Simon and Miguel laughed.
"Did you mow the lawn?" Nicole asked.
"No way!" Simon cried.
"It might end up looking like this,"
he said pointing to his head.
Now everyone laughed.

"Come on, let's play," said Joey
as he threw Simon the ball.
Simon was a FREE FISH.

the
end

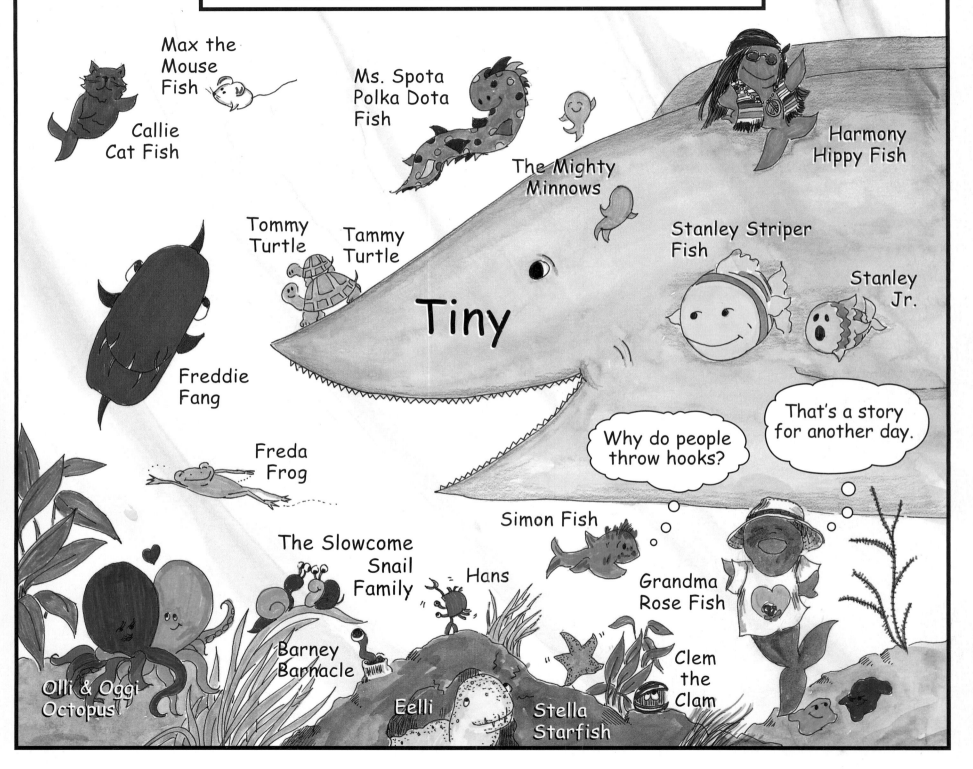

NOTE TO PARENTS AND TEACHERS:

When teased, children sometimes fall into a habit of feeling hurt, upset, and victimized. How can we help them break this pattern and learn more effective ways to handle these difficult times? Simon's Hook can help.

First, children can get so involved with the emotion of the tease that they react instinctively rather than recognize that often the sole purpose of the tease is to get a reaction. Simon's Hook compares teases to 'fishing hooks' and promotes the idea of swimming free. This offers children a different and more objective view of the teasing process.

Next, sometimes when children are teased they don't think they have options - they have to bite. When people believe they have few options they feel powerless, stuck, or controlled by others. Simon's Hook shows children many ways to swim around the hook. They see they are not powerless, they have many choices.

And last, Simon's Hook concentrates on the actions of the fish, rather than the hooks or the fishermen. This encourages children to focus on their own attitude and behavior, the only part of the interaction they control. Complaining about the other person's behavior, the cruel hook or the unfair situation is counterproductive and only leads to feelings of helplessness and self pity. By focusing on their own actions children can begin to recognize the power they have, their personal power. Personal power is not about power over someone else or the situation, but power over ourselves; our attitude, our actions, our life. An empowered attitude is instrumental in a person's ability to solve problems throughout life.

You can help too. After reading Simon's Hook you can help children recognize their choices and personal power by simply asking a question or making a comment.

- Did you bite?
- Oh, and you bit.
- I see a hook.

- Someone's been fishing.
- How can you swim free?
- Were you caught?

- Did someone throw a hook at you?
- How could you avoid that hook?
- The fish are biting today.

Encourage your child to see himself or herself as a strong and free fish with many choices, no matter what hooks the other person uses.

Karen Gedig Burnett

Karen Gedig Burnett
a.k.a. Grandma Rose

P.S. Children learn much by observing adults. How do you handle conflicts? When you're driving and someone yells at you, do you 'bite'? When someone directs a cruel comment toward you, do you get 'hooked'? Since 'actions speak louder than words,' make sure you act like a 'strong, free fish' and don't bite at other people's negative behavior.

Visit **www.grandmarose.com** for information on teasing and other books from GR Publishing.
GR Publishing   Felton, CA 95018